W9-APH-639

ATTACK OF THE ROCK MEN

BY DAVID ORME

First published in the United States in 2009
by Stone Arch Books
151 Good Counsel Drive, P.O. Box 669
Mankato, Minnesota 56002
www.stonearchbooks.com

Published by arrangement with Ransom Publishing Ltd.

Library of Congress Cataloging-in-Publication Data
Orme, David, 1948 Mar. 1–
[Boffin Boy and the Rock Men]
Attack of the Rock Men / by David Orme; illustrated by Peter Richardson.
p. cm. — (Billy Blaster)
Originally published: Boffin Boy and the Rock Men. Watlington: Ransom, 2007.
ISBN 978-1-4342-1273-3 (library binding)
1. Graphic novels. [1. Graphic novels. 2. Heroes—Fiction. 3. Science fiction.]
I. Richardson, Peter, 1965– ill. II. Title.
PZ7.7.O76Att 2009
[Fic]—dc22 2008031285

Summary:
Rock Men are the hottest new toys on the market. But when kids plug them into their computers, the toys brainwash them! Billy discovers a dangerous man is behind the sneaky plot. Can Billy Blaster and his ninja wizard friend, Wu Hoo, stop the attack of the Rock Men and save the Earth from the evil toy master?

Creative Director: Heather Kindseth
Graphic Designer: Carla Zetina-Yglesias

ATTACK OF THE ROCK MEN

s winter, and everyone
ants a Rock Man toy.
TOYS4U
STOCK!!!
ROCK MEN
NOW
IN STOCK!

ROCKMEN
ROCKMEN
ROCKMEN
Hi! I'm your Rock Man!
My name is Fred.
We will be great friends.
What is your name?

I'm your Rock Man.

I'm the perfect pet!
No need to feed me!
No need to take me for walks!

If you get bored with me, just plug me into your computer and I'll turn into someone else!

even General Bullet.
I love you, Fred.
You're such a good friend, General Bullet.

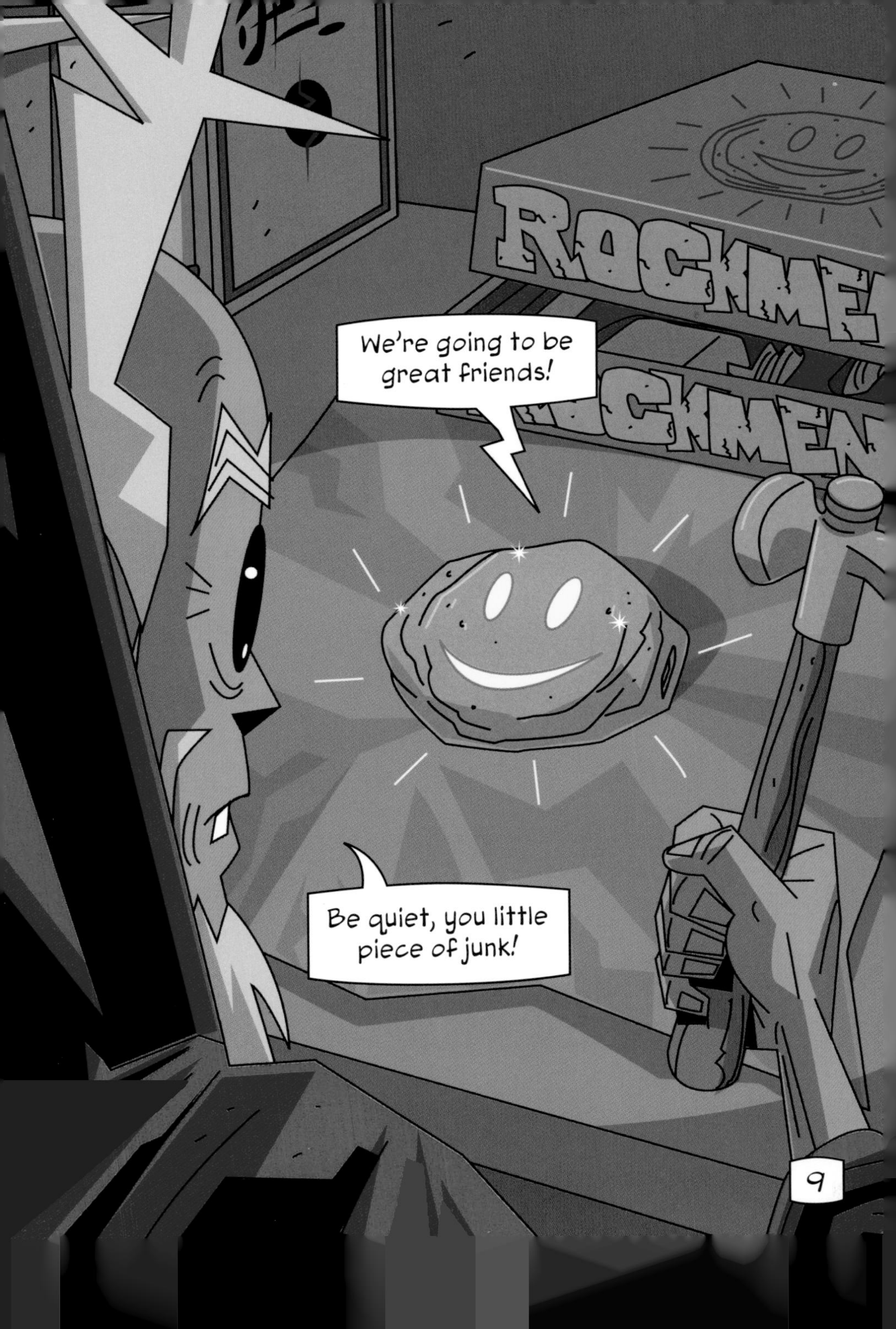
We're going to be great friends!
Be quiet, you little piece of junk!

they plug them into their computers and
turn them into new Rock Men.
CLICK!

Then something strange happens . . .
Hello, kids. I'm your friend! Go and find your parents' credit cards!

Bobby! What are you doing with my credit card?

Hurry up with that credit card number! I don't have all day!
Bobby! Call Billy Blaster right now and tell him what is happening!

Good thing you called, General! I was about to plug my Rock Man into DAVE!
Who's DAVE?

DAVE is the world's most powerful computer.
This could be serious, General. Every kid in Zone City has a Rock Man!
DAVE
KREW

Kids will be tricked if they plug their Rock Men into their computers!
By the way, why do you have a Rock Man? Aren't you too old for toys?
Um . . . I bought it for my son.

Billy calls Wu Hoo to warn him.
Wu Hoo, don't plug your Rock Man into your computer!

That won't be a
problem, Billy.

Billy goes to see Wu Hoo.
We need to find out who is doing this!
Maybe there's a clue here.

5
What does LUBRA mean?
Made just for you by LUBRA TOYS Zone City.

I know! Did you study Latin in school, Billy?
SNAP!
Nope.

LUBRA must be short for LUPUS RUBRA. That's Latin for Red Wolf!
Red Wolf is my old enemy! I should have known!
The first thing we have to do is take back all the Rock Man toys!

their Rock Men back.
If you take it away, I'll run away from home and never come back!
It's just a rock, Timmy.
PLANET NEWS
DESTROY ALL ROCKMEN!
10

Later, at the LUBRA toy factory . . .
LUBRA TOYS
Those workers have been brainwashed!
Red Wolf makes them work hard, but he doesn't pay them anything!

What should we do?
Let's get inside.
I can brainwash
people too, you know.

make more Rock Men.
Work harder!
ROCKMEN

It's over, Red Wolf!
Oh no! It's Wu Hoo and Billy Blaster!

Don't listen to Red Wolf! He has brainwashed you!
Listen to me, instead!

BZZZZZZT!
I just realized something. Red Wolf is making us work for nothing!
You're right! Red Wolf has tricked us!

into the Rock Man machine.
AAAAHH!!

I fixed all of the Rock Men toys with the help of DAVE!
Now kids can play with them without getting brainwashed!
That's too bad. You should have used the Rock Men to brainwash kids into eating their vegetables!

No way! That would be too mean.
What happened to Red Wolf?

I don't think we'll have any problems with him for a very long time!
Please get me out of here! I promise I'll be good!

ABOUT THE AUTHOR

David Orme was a teacher for 18 years before he became a full-time writer. When he is not writing books, he travels around the country, giving performances, running writing workshops, and running courses. David has written more than 250 books, including poetry collections and anthologies, fiction and nonfiction, and school text books. He lives in Winchester, England.

ABOUT THE ILLUSTRATOR

Peter Richardson's illustrations have appeared in a variety of productions and publications. He has done character designs and storyboards for many of London's top animation studios as well as artwork for advertising campaigns by big companies like BP and British Airways. His work often appears in *The Sunday Times* and *The Guardian*, as well as many magazines. He loves the Billy Blaster books and looks forward to seeing where Billy and his ninja sidekick, Wu Hoo, will end up next.

GLOSSARY

brainwash (BRAYN-wahsh)—trick someone into believing something

clue (KLOO)—something that helps you find an answer to a question or mystery

credit card (KRED-it KARD)—a small, plastic card used to pay for things

factory (FAK-tur-ree)—a building where machines are used to make products

Latin (LAT-uhn)—a language spoken in ancient Rome

machine (muh-SHEEN)—a piece of equipment used to do something

popular (POP-yuh-lur)—liked or enjoyed by many people

powerful (POU-ur-fuhl)—having great strength

realized (REE-uh-lized)—found out that something is true

tricked (TRIKD)—made someone believe something that isn't true

MORE ABOUT TOYS

The Rock Men toys were really popular with the people of Zone City. Toys have been around for thousands of years, but they are still very popular today.

Ever wonder how the teddy bear got its name? In 1902, President Theodore "Teddy" Roosevelt went on a hunting trip with his friends. The president wasn't very good at hunting, so his friends tied a bear to a tree for him to shoot. President Roosevelt said he wouldn't shoot the bear because it wasn't fair to shoot an animal that was tied up. A few years later, a toymaker named Morris Michtom heard the president's story. He decided to ask the president if he could name his toy bears "Teddy's Bears" in honor of the president. President Rooosevelt agreed, and the toymaker began selling the stuffed bears. The toy bears became really popular—so popular, in fact, that the president's daughter used many of the bears as decorations for her wedding.

AND GAMES

In the 1940s, a girl named Eleanor Abbott was sick with polio, a serious illness. Eleanor wasn't able to do much because she was so sick. She decided to create a game that other kids could play while they were sick. Her game used a board with colored spaces marked on it. For each turn, the players drew a colored card and then moved to the nearest space with the same color on it. The first person to reach the end of the board won. She called her game Candy Land. Candy Land is over 60 years old, but many children still play it today!

Frisbees are everywhere these days. It's likely that you'll see people playing with them at any park you visit. Believe it or not, Frisbees were invented by accident by bored, hungry college students! The Frisbie Baking Company sold lots of pies to students. The tins that the pies came in were shaped like today's Frisbees — round and smooth. Bored students threw the empty pie tins through the air, and before long, they were playing catch with them. It's not every day that you get to play with your food!

DISCUSSION QUESTIONS

1. In this book, Red Wolf's Rock Men toys were very popular. What are the most popular toys and games now?

2. General Bullet plays with a Rock Man toy. Is it okay for adults to have and play with toys? Why or why not?

3. Why would Red Wolf want people's credit card numbers? Why is it dangerous to give other people that information? What should the kids have done when he asked?

WRITING PROMPTS

1. On page 23, a boy's mother is trying to take away his Rock Man toy. Has anyone ever tried to take anything from you? What was it? Did you give it to them? Write about what happened.

2. Billy Blaster and Wu Hoo make a great team. Together they save Earth from Red Wolf's Rock Men. Have you ever worked with a close friend to do something? Write about it.

3. Wu Hoo uses his special powers to save the workers from Red Wolf. If you had special powers, what type of powers would you want? What would you use your special powers to do?

INTERNET SITES

Do you want to know more about subjects related to this book? Or are you interested in learning about other topics? Then check out FactHound, a fun, easy way to find Internet sites.

Our investigative staff has already sniffed out great sites for you!

Here's how to use FactHound:

1. Visit *www.facthound.com*

2. Select your grade level.

3. To learn more about subjects related to this book, type in the book's ISBN number: 9781434212733.

4. Click the Fetch It button.

FactHound will fetch the best Internet sites for you!